Mrs. Marigold's Menagerie

By Jack Gabolinscy

Illustrated by Helen Bacon

Rigby

Mrs. Marigold's Menagerie

Frost Road, where Mrs. Marigold lived, was like a centipede with a bad leg. All the houses except hers were the same – the roofs and walls were freshly painted in pale colors, the hedges neatly trimmed, the lawns mowed, and the shrubs and trees pruned to attractive shapes and sizes.

But not 27 Frost Road—Mrs. Marigold's house! Hers was the centipede's bad leg. It had a roof of striped orange and red, walls of sunbeam yellow, and windows and doors of purple. The hedges stalked around the yard with uncontrolled straggly haircuts. The lawn was waist high, and the unpruned shrubs and trees, and tangled climbing roses and jasmine made her place look like a wild Amazon jungle.

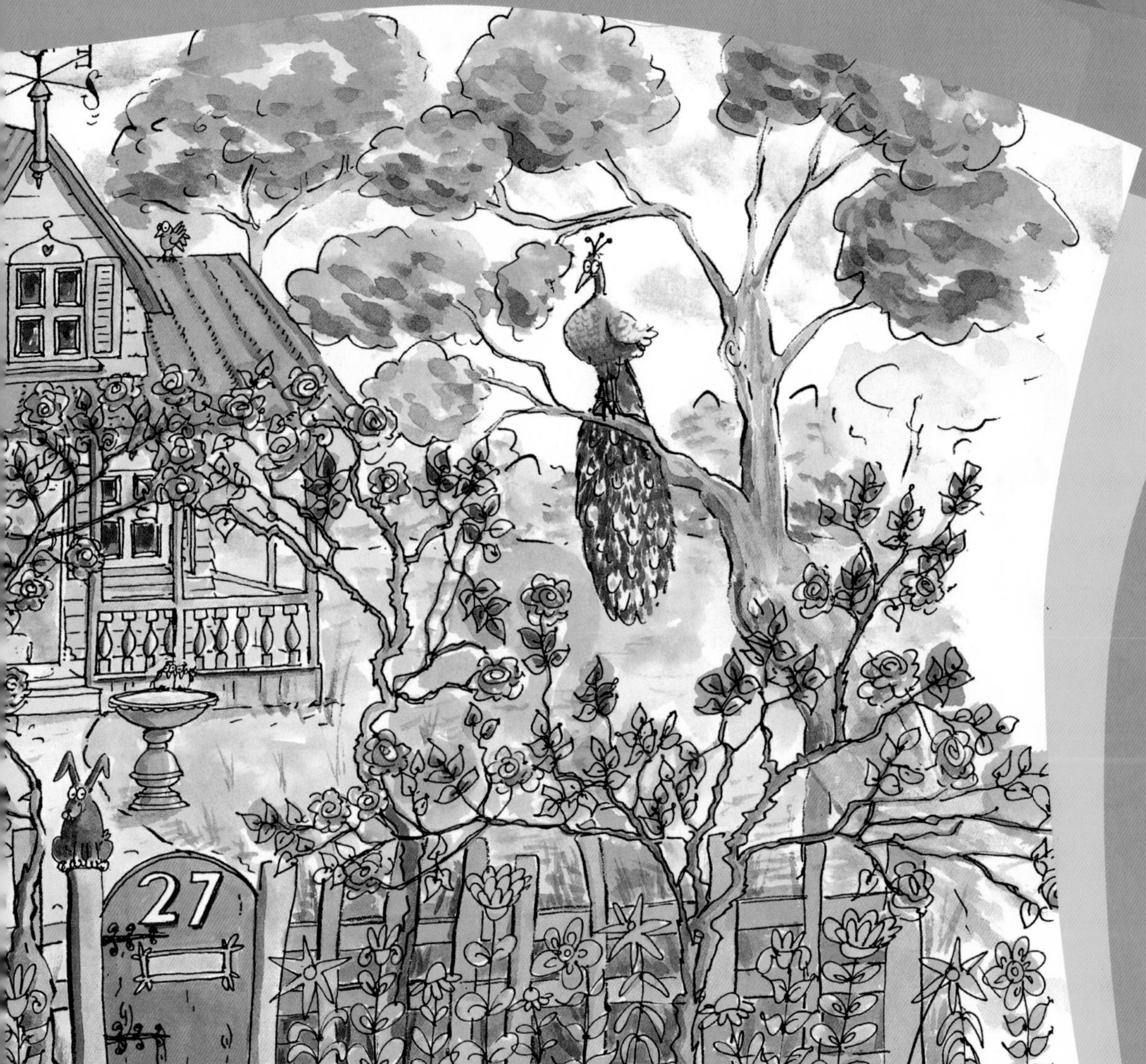
27

"That house is an ugly blot on the neighborhood," grumbled the man next door.

"Shocking!" humphed the woman across the street.

"I'm writing to the mayor," growled the woman two doors down.

"You do that," agreed her husband, flapping his arms at the peacocks in his garage.

Question:

What do you think might be in the letter to the mayor?

. . . an ugly blot

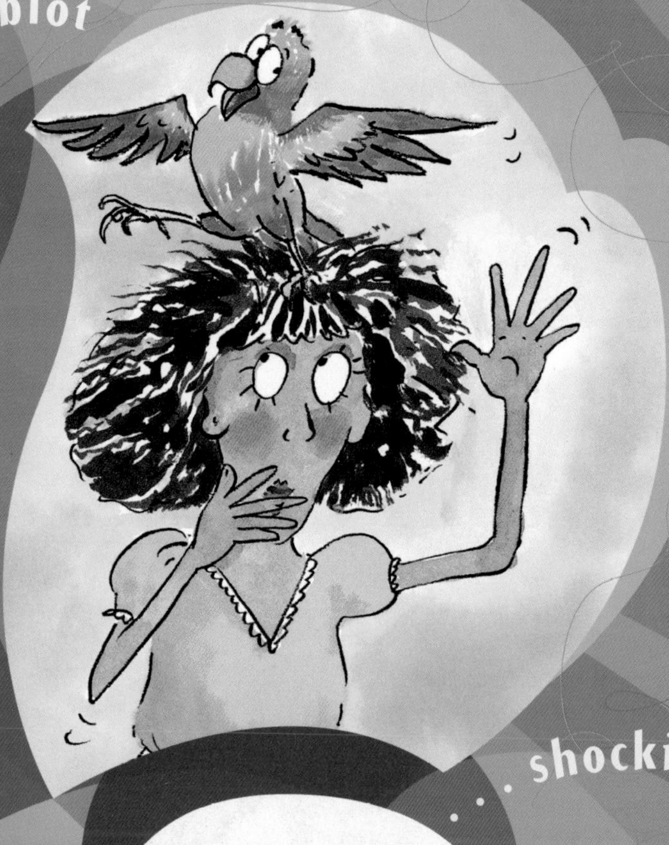

. . . shocking

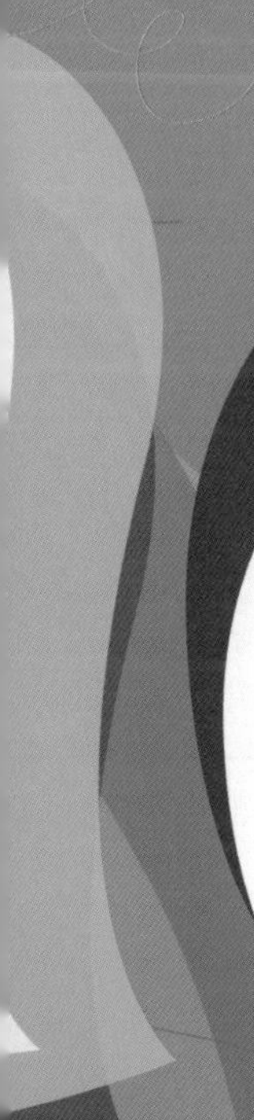

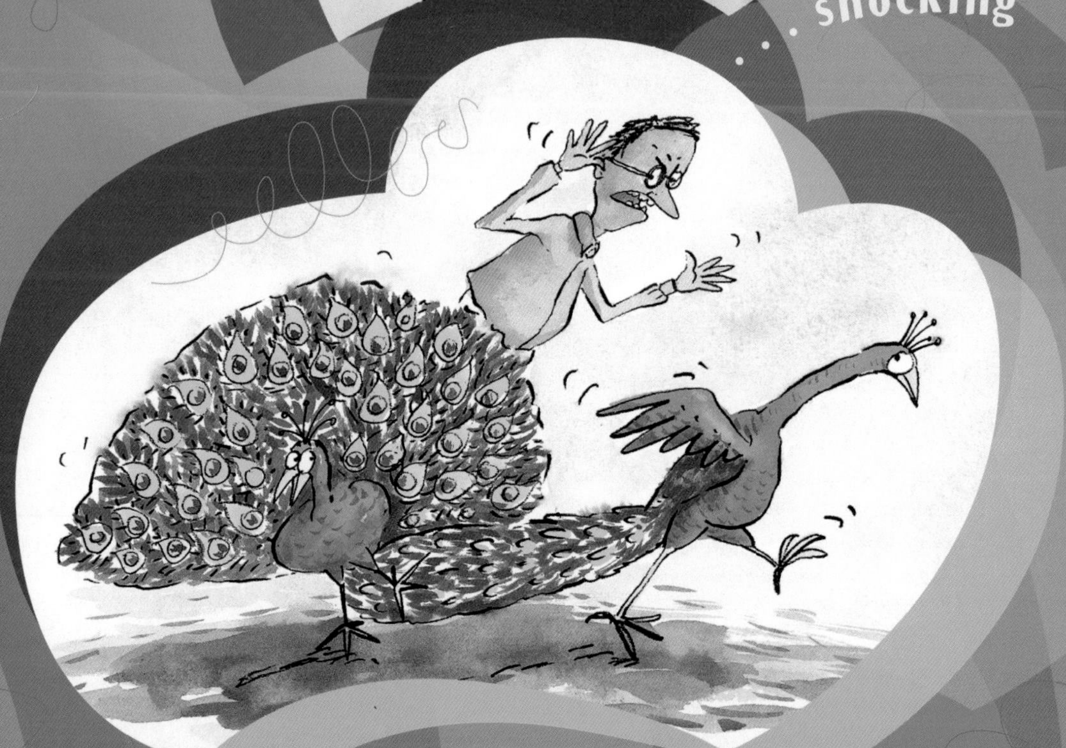

Mrs. Marigold loved her yard. "Its taken a lifetime," she said, clumping along an overgrown path in rubber boots.

And she had a large and happy "family" that lived in her yard.

There was Mop, her old terrier who was deaf. There was Slink, the cat. There was Captain Rainbow, the parrot, who screeched "Ooh yuk! Ooh yuk! Ooh yuk!" no matter what he was fed, and "Shut up! Shut up! Shut up!" whenever he was annoyed.

"Ooh yuk!
   Ooh yuk!
Shut up!
    Shut up!"

There were fish by the porch in a fish pond bright with lily flowers. And nobody knew how many rabbits and patchwork guinea pigs lived in the long grass.

Lastly, there were the peacocks, Mrs. Marigold's pride and joy. "My Royal Family," she called them.

Question:

Why do you think Mrs. Marigold called the peacocks "My Royal Family"?

Night and morning. Mrs. Marigold fed her family. Putting her fingers to her mouth, she sent a piercing whistle echoing into every nook and cranny of the neighborhood.

Every yard in the neighborhood moved. Rabbits and guinea pigs scampered home. They came from the lettuce patch down the street, from the flower beds across the street; they popped out of a hole in the nextdoor neighbor's new sunporch, and waded in from the bird bath in the yard of a house a block away. The Royal Family flew home screeching from wherever they had been roosting.

Even the sparrows and blackbirds swooped in for a meal.

Synonym:

A synonym is a word that means the same or nearly the same as another word.

Which word is the synonym for swooped?

A   dived
B   descended
C   flew

A, B, or C?

. . . . every nook

and every cranny

But one evening, after Mrs. Marigold had fed her menagerie, the telephone rang. "Mrs. Marigold, I've had enough! If you don't put your guinea pigs in a cage, I'm going to complain to the mayor. Last week they ate my spinach. Tonight they've been into my sweet peas. What will be next? Put them in cages or I will complain!"

"Shut up! Shut up! Shut up!" screeched Captain Rainbow.

"Shut up! Shut up! Shut up!"

Mrs Marigold hung up on the woman because she wasn't being polite. Soon it rang again. It was another angry neighbor.

Predict:

What do you think might happen in the story?

"Mrs. Marigold. This is Fred Oglebump from down the street. Your rabbits have just eaten my prize flowers. What are you going to do about it?"

"How do you know they were my rabbits?" asked Mrs. Marigold.

"Who else has rabbits?" shouted the man into the phone.

But Mrs. Marigold had hung up again. "Have another cracker, Captain Rainbow. If you've got nothing nice to say, don't say anything at all. That's what I say."

As you can see, Mrs. Marigold wasn't the most popular person on Frost Road. That is, unless you count the children.

Children loved her. Their teachers always brought them to visit Mrs. Marigold. They helped clean out the fish pond. They hunted through the long grass for peacock feathers, and they asked a hundred and one questions.

"Can I borrow a guinea pig for the school fair?"

"How do you teach a parrot to talk?"

"How many feathers are in a peacock's tail?"

Inference:

"Children loved her."

What inferences can you make from this text about Mrs. Marigold's character?

One morning, while Mrs. Marigold was feeding her family, a very angry man stormed onto her porch. He waved his arms and shouted, "Those birds! They have messed on my car!"

"Calm yourself, Mr. Symes. You will give yourself a heart attack. Can I make you a cup of coffee?" asked Mrs. Marigold.

"No! I don't want a cup of coffee! I want those grubby birds!" shouted the man, and he stepped toward the peacocks.

"ScreeEEeech!! ScreeEEEeech!! Shut up! Shut up!" squawked Captain Rainbow, flying at the man's face.

"ScreeEEEeech!!"

"ScreeEEEeech!!"

14

... I want those grubby birds!

Back stepped the man off the porch – a perfect backward dive – into the fish pond. He stood up, dripping water and leaves from his hair and clothes.

"Ooh yuk! Ooh yuk! Ooh yuk!" cackled Captain Rainbow.

The man fled from the fish pond toward the gate. "You've left your hat, Mr. Symes," called Mrs. Marigold, but he didn't come back.

Action and Consequence:

The man stepped back off the porch.	The man fell into the fish pond.

Find another action and consequence.

A few days later, Mrs. Marigold received a letter from the mayor. It said:

Dear Mrs. Marigold,
Your neighbors have complained about your untidy yard and your wild animals.

One man has had his prize flowers eaten by your rabbits and guinea pigs. Others say your garden is an eyesore. Another man tells me he was attacked by a screaming bird and chased into a pond. He says your peacocks are always messing on his car.

As mayor, it is my job to look after our town's good name and to make sure every citizen is safe. I would like to visit you on Tuesday afternoon to investigate these serious complaints.

The Mayor,
Mr. Archibald Snooks

"How nice," said Mrs. Marigold to herself. "A visit from the mayor. We must see that he has a good time."

Problem and Solution:

| Mrs Marigold's neighbors have complaints. | ? |

How do you think the problem could be solved?

That afternoon, Mrs. Marigold did three jobs.

First, she called Sunnyside School and spoke to the principal.

Then she watered her yard with "Blush", the plant food for fantastically fast-blooming and fragrant flowers.

Lastly, she made herself a cup of coffee and took Captain Rainbow on her knee. "I've been meaning to talk to you about your manners for a while now, Captain Rainbow," she said.

On Tuesday, when the mayor arrived, a crowd of people gathered across the road to welcome him. They clapped and cheered as he got out of his car.

Everybody was happy. The bad leg on the centipede was at last going to be cleaned up.

But at Mrs. Marigolds' . . .

Alliteration:

Repetition of initial sounds that creates a noticeable effect.

Which example of text includes alliteration?

A ... she called Sunnyside School and spoke to the principal

B ... food for fantastically fast-blooming and fragrant flowers

A or B?

. . . Mrs. Marigold's yard was in glorious bloom. The air was alive with perfumes and the singing of the birds.

In the long grass, children fed and played with rabbits and guinea pigs. The Royal Family spread its feathers in a brilliant display of color.

The mayor, back straight and stern, walked up the sidewalk.

"Hello, Mr. Mayor. Lovely day. Hello, Mr. Mayor. Lovely day," called Captain Rainbow from the porch.

Mrs. Marigold sat on the porch in the middle of an excited group of children.

"What is a rabbit's favorite food?"

"How long do parrots live?"

"How big do goldfish grow?"

Antonym:

An antonym is a word that means the opposite of another word.

Which word is the antonym for brilliant?

A dull
B beautiful
C ordinary

A, B, or C?

The mayor talked to Mrs. Marigold, he talked to the children, and he talked to their teacher. He asked all sorts of questions. He looked into untrimmed hedges and unpruned trees. He walked through tangled grass and vines and tried to count the number of animals in the yard. He stayed for a whole hour.

Captain Rainbow perched on the mailbox as the mayor climbed into his car. "Goodbye, Sir! Drive carefully! Goodbye, Sir! Drive carefully!" he called.

Character Profile:

Which words would you use to describe the character of Mrs. Marigold?

bossy

creative

mean

gentle

calm

prejudiced

The whole street waited for the mayor's decision. "Won't it be wonderful?" asked the woman down the street. "No more untidy lawns, no more bedraggled hedges or ugly trees, no more nasty rabbits and guinea pigs, no more messy peacocks. Won't our street be perfect!"

On Thursday morning, a yellow city government van pulled up at the gate. A workman nailed a big white board to the lamppost. He put a letter into Mrs. Marigold's mailbox and then drove off.

"Look!" called the man in the house across the street. "Mrs. Marigold got her marching orders from the mayor."

"I'll bet it's a tidy-up-or-leave notice," said Mr. Oglebump.

"I hope it's a demolition notice," grumbled Mr. Symes. But it wasn't either of these. The sign said:

PROTECTED
All animals and plants
in this yard
are protected
by law.
The Mayor

PROTECTED

All animals and plants
in this yard
are protected
by law.
The Mayor

Question:
Why do you think the mayor wanted to protect Mrs. Marigold's yard?

That afternoon, when the children came visiting, Mrs. Marigold showed them the sign and read the letter she had received.

Dear Mrs. Marigold,

Thank you for the wonderful afternoon I spent looking at your yard. Your yard is different, but it is beautiful. I have decided to make it a nature Reserve so that all the plants and animals are protected.

I will visit again soon. Your yard makes me stop thinking about all the hard work I've got to do. We can talk about how to stop your pets from straying and upsetting your neighbors.

Your friend,
Archibald Snooks (The Mayor)

When evening came, Mrs. Marigold put her fingers to her mouth and sent out an ear-splitting whistle. It echoed into every nook and cranny in the neighborhood. Home came the rabbits and guinea pigs. Home came the peacocks.

Home to celebrate.

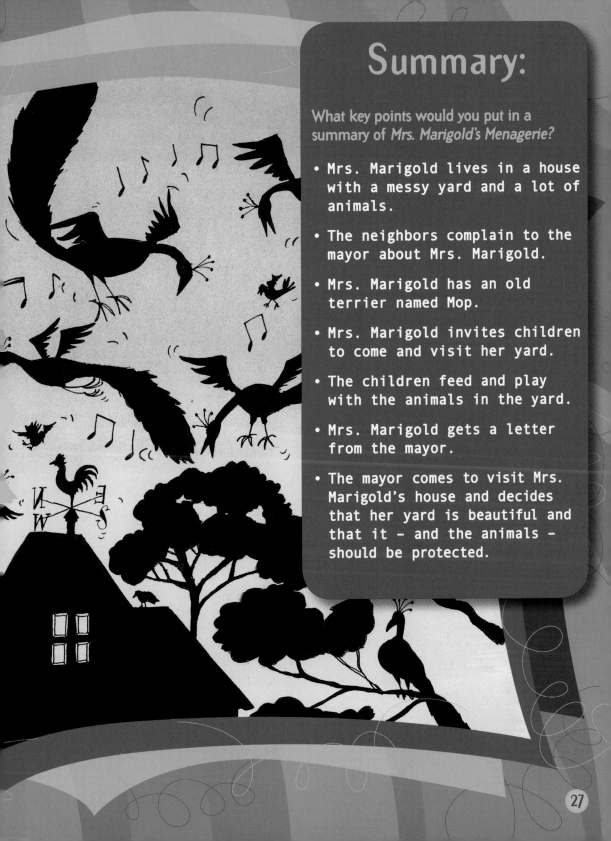

Summary:

What key points would you put in a summary of *Mrs. Marigold's Menagerie?*

- Mrs. Marigold lives in a house with a messy yard and a lot of animals.

- The neighbors complain to the mayor about Mrs. Marigold.

- Mrs. Marigold has an old terrier named Mop.

- Mrs. Marigold invites children to come and visit her yard.

- The children feed and play with the animals in the yard.

- Mrs. Marigold gets a letter from the mayor.

- The mayor comes to visit Mrs. Marigold's house and decides that her yard is beautiful and that it – and the animals – should be protected.

Think about the Text

Making connections — talk about the connections you can make to the story, *Mrs. Marigold's Menagerie*.

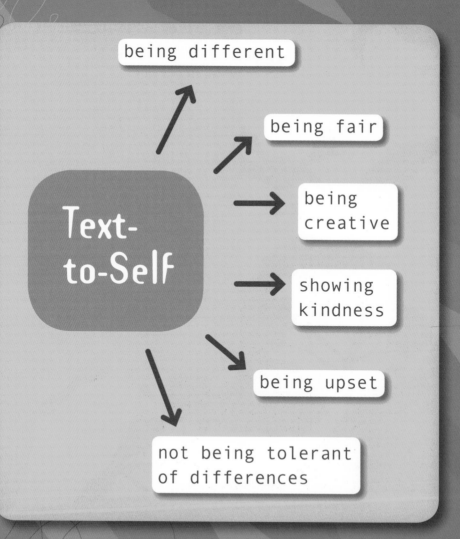

being different

being fair

Text-to-Self

being creative

showing kindness

being upset

not being tolerant of differences

Text-to-Text

Talk about other stories you may have read that have similar features. Compare the stories.

Text-to-World

Talk about situations in the world that might connect to elements in the story.

Planning a Short Story

1 ## Decide on a storyline

Mrs. Marigold has problems with her neighbors, who do not like her messy yard and her many animals.

→

The neighbors complain about Mrs. Marigold to the mayor, and he plans a visit to her house to check things out.

→

Mrs. Marigold invites all her friends to visit on the same day, and gives her yard plant food so it will be in full bloom.

The major visits and talks to the children and Mrs. Marigold. He is very impressed by the yard and animals.

→

The mayor makes Mrs. Marigold's yard a Nature Reserve to protect it by law.

2 ## Think about the characters

Think about the way they will think, act, and feel. Make some short notes or quick sketches.

Mrs. Marigold	Neighbors	The Mayor

creative kind eccentric	prejudiced judgemental unforgiving	fair supportive responsible

3 Decide on setting or settings
Make some short notes.

4 Decide on the events in order

Mrs. Marigold's neighbors complain about her messy yard and animals.

Introduction

Events

The neighbors write a letter of complaint to the mayor.

Conclusion

Short stories usually have . . .

A A short introduction that grabs the reader's interest

B Fewer characters than longer stories

C A single fast-moving plot

D A climax that occurs late in the story